This Book
Belongs To:

....

....

Stories for **Five** Year Olds

Stories for
Five
Year Olds

PaRragon

Bath • New York • Singapore • Hong Kong • Cologne • Delhi
Melbourne • Amsterdam • Johannesburg • Auckland • Shenzhen

Illustrated by Claire Henley

First published by Parragon in 2011

Parragon
Queen Street House
4 Queen Street
Bath BA1 1HE, UK

ISBN 978-1-4454-1989-3

Printed in China

Contents

Rocky Finds a New Job

"Hooray! It's Saturday!" yelled Tom and Jenny as they ran up to the little ice cream parlor in the park, where Rocky the Dinosaur worked.

Everyone liked Rocky and he was always happy, serving all the children in the ice cream parlor.

After an ice cream each, Tom and Jenny played on the swings.

"Wheee!" they yelled excitedly, as they pumped higher and higher.

Just then, Mr. Gribble, the head of the park, put a sign on the monkey bars.

"Sorry kids," he said, "this isn't safe any more, but don't worry, we're getting a brand new one next week!"

Jenny and Tom went to tell Rocky the exciting news, and eventually found Rocky sitting alone on a bench, looking unhappy.

"What's wrong, Rocky?" they asked.

"Well, the new monkey bars are very expensive. There's not enough money to buy them and keep the ice cream parlor open too. So I have to look for a new job," replied Rocky, looking even sadder.

"We'll miss you so much," said Jenny, almost crying.

Luckily, on his way home, Rocky passed a museum, where they needed a dinosaur for a new exhibit.

MUSEUM

Dinosaur wanted — apply within

"It doesn't sound as fun as the ice cream parlor," thought Rocky. "But I'll give it a try, anyway."

The next week, Tom and Jenny went to the park. The new monkey bars were coming that very afternoon.

All of a sudden, Mr. Gribble came rushing up. "Something terrible has happened!" he said.

"What's wrong?" asked Tom and Jenny.

"I've just heard that the new monkey bars have fallen apart. It's a disaster! Everyone will be so upset!" he said unhappily. Just then, Tom had an idea. He grabbed Jenny by the hand.

They raced into town, and ran straight into the museum. They found Rocky standing very still in one of the rooms.

Rocky's eyes lit up when he saw Tom and Jenny.

"Hello, Tom! Hello, Jenny!" he exclaimed. "What are you doing here?"

"Come with us, we've got an idea!" said Tom, quickly grabbing Rocky's hand, as people looked on in amazement.

Back at the park, the children ran straight up to Mr. Gribble.

"I've had a great idea!" said Tom. "Why can't Rocky be our new monkey bars?"

"Oh, please!" cried Jenny. "It's a great idea, and will make everyone so happy."

They waited for his answer, hardly daring to breathe.

"I think it's a wonderful idea, too," said Mr. Gribble. "Welcome back, Rocky!"

Everyone cheered loudly, especially Rocky.

Molly and Moonlight

Of all her toys, Molly's favorite was her little horse, Moonlight. She was pale silver, and her eyes sparkled like stars.

Molly and Moonlight had wonderful pretend adventures.

Molly loved Moonlight. But more than anything, she wished that Moonlight could be a real pony, who would prance and gallop, and take her on real adventures.

One night, not long after Molly fell asleep, a soft whooshing noise woke her up. She sat up in bed and saw that her window was open, and the wind was blowing the curtain.

In the shimmering moonlight, Molly noticed something that made her heart stop...

Moonlight was gone! Jumping out of bed, Molly rushed to the window and looked out. She could hardly believe her eyes! There, prancing around the apple tree in the middle of the backyard, was Moonlight.

Filled with wonder and excitement, Molly rushed downstairs. She let herself out of the back door and ran into the backyard.

With Molly on her back, Moonlight trotted around the backyard. Then she began to gallop and, with a quick leap, sailed over the fence.

Molly held her breath and clung to Moonlight's silver mane as they galloped.

Suddenly, it felt as if Moonlight was galloping on the wind itself.

Looking down, Molly realized that they were flying in the wind, across the midnight sky.

Higher and higher they flew, above the rooftops and treetops. The full moon cast its silvery beams, and all around them the stars twinkled merrily.

With a prance, Moonlight took Molly swooping through the stars and clouds. They leapt over moonbeams, darted between shooting stars, and raced around planets.

When the first light of dawn began painting the sky pink, Molly knew it was time to go home.

Moonlight flew down, into the garden and in through Molly's bedroom window.

Molly crawled into bed, and fell fast asleep.

Soon sunlight was streaming through the window, and Molly's mom was calling from downstairs.

"Molly, it's time to get up!"

Molly looked over at the window-sill. There was Moonlight, just where she always was.

"Was I just dreaming?" Molly wondered. She rushed to the window and looked down into the backyard. Everything looked the same, but…were those really hoofprints around the apple tree?

Molly looked at Moonlight. Maybe it was the breeze blowing Moonlight's mane, or maybe Molly's eyes were playing tricks on her. But she was sure Moonlight was gently nodding at her!

No Such Thing as Magic

Joshua looked like an ordinary little boy. But Joshua wasn't ordinary at all. You see, Joshua was a wizard. A wizard who could do all sorts of magical things…like turning dogs into toads, and cabbages into cake!

Joshua always tried his best to show his mom and dad what a wonderful wizard he was, but they were usually too busy being grown-ups to pay attention.

And whenever they did notice, they'd always say, with a laugh,

"Joshua, don't be silly. There's no such thing as magic!"

Not even Joshua's friends believed he was a wizard. They thought he was joking. Even when he made delicious cookies and sandwiches appear for them to eat.

Then, on Joshua's birthday, he had a huge party at his house with all his friends.

"I'll show you I'm a wizard," cried Joshua. "I'll change Mom's party food into a feast."

Throwing his arms wide open, Joshua shouted, "Abracadabra!"

In a flash, the table was piled high with incredible cakes, amazing cookies, and tons of candy. In the center of the table was an enormous chocolate-frosted birthday cake.

"Yesssss!" cheered all the children, digging in greedily.

"Wow," burped Sam. "So you really are a wizard, after all."

"Yes," replied Joshua, looking very happy with himself. "And to prove it even more, I'm going to bring in some of my special friends."

Joshua stood back and clapped his hands three times. In a puff of magic smoke, Martha the Monster and Dermot the Dragon appeared before them. Martha and Dermot were the cuddliest, friendliest, nicest creatures you could wish to meet, and before long, everyone was getting along.

Dermot had a great time giving the children rides around the room, and then Martha showed them all how to do the monster stomp. Everyone squealed with laughter as they thumped around the dining room while Dermot tapped out the beat with his tail.

Then, suddenly, over all the noise, Joshua heard a door slam. His mom was coming back. Quick as a flash, he clapped his hands and Martha and Dermot disappeared. By the time the door swung open, all the children were sitting back around the table once more.

"What was all that noise about?" frowned Mom.

"Nothing," cried all the children at once.

And Mom soon forgot all about the noise when she saw their empty plates. "Amazing," she beamed. "Looks like you all enjoyed that."

"Yes," cried Joshua and his friends. They certainly had enjoyed their magical afternoon.

And from that day on, Joshua's friends never forgot that he was an amazing wizard. But they all agreed that the grown-ups should never be told, because, after all, grown-ups think "there's no such thing as magic!"

Elephant Has a Cold

It was a peaceful morning in the jungle. Everything was calm and quiet. Until…AH-CHOO-BOOOOOM!

The loud crash echoed through the jungle, rattling the treetops and making the ground tremble. Coconuts toppled down and rolled everywhere.

It happened again and again. Trees shook, and large rocks began sliding into the river.

"This is awful!" said Hippo.

"We have to cure Elephant's cold," said Giraffe.

"Warm coconut milk can be very soothing," said Monkey, opening a coconut.

Elephant stuck out his trunk and tried to drink some of the milk.

Slip-slurp…

AH-CHOO-BOOOOM!

A great big sneeze sent the coconut milk flying, splashing over everyone else.

Elephant sniffled miserably. "I've nebber had a tode before," he said.

"I dust want to feel bedder!"

"Why don't you try a nice soothing mud bath?" asked Hippo.

Everyone thought that sounded like a good idea.

"Berry relaxig!" said Elephant, as he sank into the squidgy mud.

Everyone else was beginning to relax, too, as they watched Elephant sink down deeper into the mud with a happy smile on his face.

"Ahhh," sighed Elephant contentedly. "Ahhh… ahhh…AH-CHOO-BOOOOOM!"

Elephant's sneeze splattered mud all over his friends.

"It's no use," said Parrot, shaking the mud out of her feathers. "We'll have to call Dr. Lion."

"Where's the patient?" Dr. Lion asked importantly, when he arrived. The animals led him to Elephant, who was sitting miserably with some palm leaves wrapped around his trunk.

"Hmmm…" said Dr. Lion, listening to Elephant's chest.

"Say ahhh," said Dr. Lion, looking at Elephant's throat.

"I see," said Dr. Lion, looking in Elephant's ears. "Yes, indeed," said Dr. Lion, looking down Elephant's trunk.

"Well," said Dr. Lion, after he had finished examining Elephant, "the only thing that will cure Elephant's bad cold is…"

The other animals came closer to listen.

"…rest!" announced Dr. Lion. "Lots of rest is the only cure for a cold in the trunk."

As soon as Dr. Lion left, Elephant fell fast asleep. He slept for the rest of the day…and all that night…and all the next day and night, too.

His friends took turns sitting with him so they could be sure he was all right. He snuffled and snorted, and snored, but he didn't sneeze. Not once!

On the third morning, Elephant woke up, stretched his trunk, and took a deep breath…

"Ah…ah…"

All his friends held their breath…

"…Aaaaaaahhhh! I feel SO much better!" Elephant announced.

The other animals cheered and hugged Elephant.

"We're so glad!" they said.

"Thank you all for looking after me," said Elephant. "You've been such good friends. And, of course, I would do the same for you if any of you had a cold!"

"That's good," said Parrot, "because I think… SQUAWK-CHOOOOOO! I may be next!"

Ella's Playhouse

One hot summer's day, Ella found her dad snoozing in his deckchair.

"Dad," she called out. "I'd really like a playhouse in the backyard. Will you build me one?" Ella's dad woke up and said sleepily, "Of course, Ella, anything you like."

"Will it be ready by this afternoon?" asked Ella, shaking him by the arm.

"Well, Ella, making a playhouse is not as easy as all that!" he explained. "First we'll have to draw a picture of what we want it to look like, and then..."

"That's okay, Dad. I know exactly how I want it!" said Ella. "I'll go and get my crayons."

After a while, they had finished the drawing of the playhouse. It had pink walls, four little windows, and a bright red front door.

26

It also had curtains and a white fence around the outside.

"That's exactly right!" beamed Ella. "Now, when will it be ready?"

"Well, Ella, it's not as easy as all that," he explained. "I'll have to find some wood to make the walls and roof, and..."

"That's okay, Dad. There is some wood in the shed. I'll help you get it."

Ella dragged him by the hand to the shed.

After an hour, they had collected enough wood. Ella's dad was now very hot, dirty, dusty, and covered in cobwebs! He was also exhausted and sat down on the sofa for a break.

"Dad, does this mean you've finished my playhouse?" Ella asked, popping her head around the door a little while later.

"Ah, well now, um…I just came in to find some of my tools…" said Dad.

"I know exactly where your tool box is," said Ella. "Come with me and I'll show you."

Dad reluctantly followed her into the garage. There, on his work bench, was a big box of tools.

"Thank you, Ella," said Dad. "Now I'll be able to start building your playhouse."

Rolling up his sleeves, he took out some tools and started building. For the rest of the afternoon, he hammered and sawed, screwed and painted, until, just as it was getting dark, he had finished the playhouse. It looked just like Ella's drawing!

"Ella will be so happy!" Dad said to himself.

Tired, he collected up his tools and carried the heavy box back to the house.

"I wonder where Ella is?" thought Dad.

He went into the living room, and there was Ella, fast asleep on the sofa.

"Ella," he called gently. "Wake up, Ella, your playhouse is finished!"

Ella slowly opened her eyes and yawned loudly.

"Dad," she said, "I've just had the best dream about a big swimming pool in the backyard! Please can you build me one of those now?"